Sha'Tanya

UNLEASHED

Sha'Tanya
UNLEASHED

MARIO HERBERT

CONTENTS

Introduction vii

The Seat 1

Error! 21

Endgame 39

INTRODUCTION

This is the story of Sha'Tanya Carter, a gel abusing, street-smart, thirteen-year-old girl, first introduced in the Adrian series of books.

She was first seen in *Adrian at Large*, and formally introduced by name in *Adrian at Last*. She went on to play a major role in the rest of the series, but now, it's time for Sha'Tanya to take centre stage.

Intriguing adventures and painful lessons await you in the stories that follow, which all predate the events of the Adrian series.

No prior reading is required to thoroughly enjoy this rich, new extension to the Adrian universe so turn the page and let the adventures begin!

THE SEAT

The early morning breeze blew an empty snack wrapper along a busy road, in front of a hospital on the outskirts of the city. Just as the wrapper reached a bus stop in front of the hospital, its motion was cut short by the wheel of a car, which stopped directly on top of it. The back passenger side door opened and a dark, slim, but shapely girl exited—Sha'Tanya was on the scene. She thanked the driver and closed the door, taking a brief moment to examine her appearance in the reflection of the tinted window of the blue sedan before it started to move again.

"Hair gel on point," she thought, as she glanced at her glistening hair which was immobilised by an overly generous allowance of hair gel.

"Hotter than a kettle in a house fire," she thought, as she glanced with approval at the way her uniform subjected her body to a bear hug. She couldn't wait to start her day—and hopefully, run into a certain boy on the bus.

Finally, she turned around to face the bus stop, as the car drove off. There was a tall, thick, dark girl with corn rows at the bus stop in the same red and white uniform Sha'Tanya was wearing.

"Sha'Tanya Carter has landed!" Sha'Tanya announced, smugly, as she struck a pose and smiled at the other girl.

"You think you're so hot," said the girl.

"Laurel, Laurel, Laurel," replied Sha'Tanya, shaking her head. "Error! I don't think I'm hot; I know I'm hot!"

Laurel laughed heartily.

"I had to walk all the way from the bus yard up here," said Laurel, folding her arms, "you got a ride!"

"Well excuse me for being persuasive!" cried Sha'Tanya, cutting her eyes at Laurel.

"Hmmm," muttered Laurel, "this plan of yours had better be worth it."

Sha'Tanya paused for a moment.

"This girl questioning me for real?" she thought to herself as she gave Laurel a critical look.

"I've had a seat every morning for the past week," said Sha'Tanya, finally, raising her hands in a defensive posture, "ain't no error in my plan—catch the bus from outside the 'horsepital' before it gets into town, and get a seat before anybody else can board."

"Is this gonna cost us another bus fare?" asked Laurel, with a worried look on her face.

Sha'Tanya put her arm akimbo, as she processed Laurel's question.

"This girl thinks I'm paying bus fare from the

'horsepital' to town, and then from town to school?" she thought, before verbalizing her thought in a single word.

"Error!" cried Sha'Tanya. "The conductor knows full well that my destination is school—not town!"

Suddenly, a sound caught Sha'Tanya's ear, and a smile invaded her face.

"That's the ride coming!" cried Sha'Tanya, with excitement.

"I will never understand how you can tell one bus from the next," started Laurel, shaking her head and staring at Sha'Tanya intently, "just from hearing the sound of the engine."

"Simple," replied Sha'Tanya, looking at Laurel condescendingly, "the engines don't growl the same way; that growl belongs to *Turbulence*, my dear."

In short order, a bus came barrelling around the corner, and approached the bus stop with speed. It was adorned with spoilers, decorative roof racks, side skirts and decorative window tints. Under the front license plate, the word "Turbulence" was airbrushed; this was the name of the bus.

Laurel stepped forward and extended her hand, signalling the driver to stop. As the bus prepared to stop, Sha'Tanya just slightly shook her head.

"No need to stop the bus, Laurel," said Sha'Tanya, with a calm smugness, "that's 'Count Dracula' driving; he knows to stop for me."

The bus stopped, the door opened in front of Sha'Tanya and a clear, tall and lanky conductor with unkempt shrubbery for hair, hung his body through it, signalling the girls to come. He wore a shabby, washed-out, yellow, blue and black uniform, which looked more like multigenerational hand-me-down rags.

"Step up there, sweet girl," said the conductor as Sha'Tanya mounted the steps, beaming with joy at the conductor's affectionate greeting.

"You coming here, too, 'Thickness'," he said, calling to Laurel, who promptly followed in Sha'Tanya's footsteps.

The door closed behind Laurel and the bus jolted off towards the city. Sha'Tanya basked in the glory of the moment as she made her way through the colourfully airbrushed interior of the bus, pushing through the large crowd of passengers. All was going according to plan; she had managed to get a ride to the hospital bus stop, meet Laurel and board the bus of her choice within the expected timeframe. Soon, she would be in the bus yard, and as her schoolmates waited for passengers to disembark, she would take up her place in the seat of her choosing.

To Sha'Tanya's delight, the bell was pressed, and a couple proceeded to disembark the bus at the very next bus stop. Apart from Sha'Tanya and Laurel, all of the standing passengers were disembarking in the nearby city, and showed no interest in occupying the back seats which had just been vacated. Sha'Tanya and Laurel availed themselves of the now vacant seats, which were serendipitously next to each other in the left corner of the very back of the bus.

As Count Dracula revved the engine to move off, Sha'Tanya beamed with triumph. The sponge of the seat felt better in that moment than she remembered it ever feeling. Unfortunately, that triumph was about to be stripped away.

As the bus moved off, the driver pushed the button to close the door, as usual. However, on this occasion, as the hinged door started to straighten out, the outer half of the door became loose, dropping off its hinges, and falling out of the doorway, onto the sidewalk. The driver stopped the bus immediately and Sha'Tanya, looking through the window, witnessed the conductor hop out to retrieve the half of the door which had dropped off. Sha'Tanya then listened in horror as the conductor stepped back into the bus with the half-door, and was informed of the next course of action by the driver.

"'Red Man', we gotta drop these people in the bus yard and then carry the bus off the road to get that door fixed!"

Sha'Tanya's world was shattered; she couldn't believe what she was hearing.

"Guess we have to fight for a seat after all," said Laurel, with a sigh, as the sign was changed to "Private" and the bus started off again.

Sha'Tanya replayed that morning's events in her mind. She couldn't accept that all of her efforts so far would count for nothing, and this was verbalised in a single word.

"Error!" she cried as she jumped up and pressed the bell.

"We're getting off?" asked Laurel with a puzzled expression.

"You think I'm letting them carry me in the bus yard to fight with those simpletons?" replied Sha'Tanya, staring at Laurel as though she were mad.

"Hey," cried Laurel, as the girls rose to make their way forward in the bus, "not long ago, we used to be with those 'simpletons' fighting for a seat!"

"Ain't nothing wrong with being a fool," started Sha'Tanya, as the girls made their way through the crowd, "but according to my grandmother, to stay a fool is a critical error."

Shortly after, Sha'Tanya and Laurel were deposited at the next bus stop, by a big public park, surrounded by tall hedges. The bus yard wasn't far away.

"Sorry, sweet girl," said Red Man to Sha'Tanya as she exited.

Sha'Tanya and Laurel now stood at a bus stop with a host of other girls and boys from their school, who had just been turned away from boarding *Turbulence*. Sha'Tanya explained to the group—who all knew her—what had just happened with the door.

"At least we can still get a bus before it hits the bus yard," said Laurel, as she looked up the street.

"This ain't a safe place to wait," whispered Sha'Tanya, as she nervously looked around, "we got to get out of here—fast."

Laurel stared at Sha'Tanya with her arms akimbo and discombobulation etched upon her face. Sha'Tanya was about to render an explanation but just then, the sound of a siren pierced her ears.

Sha'Tanya grabbed Laurel's hand and pulled her through the crowd of children. She then dashed through a small opening in the hedge, leading into the public park, and crouched down behind the hedge, dragging Laurel with her. Sha'Tanya's heart was beating like a hammer pounding a nail into hard wood. Laurel had a look of confusion on her face, but Sha'Tanya knew exactly what was happening.

On the other side of the hedge were truancy officers, tasked with rounding up delinquent children and getting them to school by any means, including the white van, in which they travelled. Sha'Tanya fully intended to attend school, but by her preferred means—not theirs. From her crouched position, she overheard a female student on the other side of the hedge, attempting to sell her out.

"Wait a minute, Sha'Tanya Carter was here just now," said the girl on the other side, "officer, she and her friend must have slipped into the park!"

"Stinking Emelia Harris," Sha'Tanya muttered under her breath as she gripped Laurel's hand firmly and darted off along the inside of the hedge.

A few moments later, a bony man of medium height in a green uniform, burst through the hedges and started to visually survey the park. He was extremely dark in complexion, with bushy white sideburns culminating in a short, white beard, which extended down his neck and onto his chest. His sideburns continued up, into a low crown of white hair around the top of his head, leaving a shiny patch of bald, dark scalp in the middle.

"My word," whispered Sha'Tanya, as she peeped at him from behind a tall garbage can, "he looks like a green monkey with a bald patch."

Laurel gave a chuckle from behind an adjacent can. There was a huge obelisk-shaped monument in the near distance, with a wide base.

"When that bald-patched monkey looks away," whispered Sha'Tanya to Laurel, "make a run for the monument."

As soon as the man looked away, the girls darted from behind the cans and headed for the monument. Sha'Tanya's heart raced like a horse in a derby, rivalled only by her feet. Finally, the girls reached the monument and crouched down behind it, each taking a moment to catch their breath.

"Think he saw us?" asked Laurel.

"Too afraid to look," replied Sha'Tanya, trying to find the brake pedal for her heart.

Finally, she made a quick glance, and gave up the search for the brake.

"We gotta move now!" she cried as she grabbed Laurel's hand and dashed off; the green monkey had seen them and was in pursuit.

Sha'Tanya knew she had to think quickly. She surveyed the park as she ran; there was a playground, various trees, benches and a set of bathrooms.

"He can't follow us into the girls' bathroom," she thought to herself, "I'll scream louder than a pig at the slaughterhouse."

Sha'Tanya dashed deep into the bathroom, dragging Laurel behind her. Once there, the girls took a moment to collect themselves.

The bathroom consisted of a straight corridor,

sandwiched between a row of stalls and a row of sinks set in a long counter. Above the sinks was a long mirror, spanning the entire length of the counter. The back wall of the bathroom had a single, small window, set close to the ceiling, in the middle of the central corridor. The girls stood, resting their hands on the counter, looking head-on into the mirror at each other.

"Now what?" asked Laurel.

"I don't know, but I know I ain't going to school in a truant van, nor in one of those rust-bucket buses," replied Sha'Tanya, in a defiant tone, "I have to get out of this bathroom and get to a bus stop before *The Road Warrior* passes."

"Really?" asked Laurel, turning her head to look directly at Sha'Tanya. "The children from 'Dead Sea High' take that bus; our children take *Turbulence*."

"The school's real name is South Sea Secondary," quipped Sha'Tanya, in a highly defensive tone, "and some of those children do ride *Turbulence*; you telling me I can't ride *The Road Warrior*?"

"Hardly any South Sea children ride *Turbulence*," cried Laurel, defending her position firmly, "I can count them on one hand—wait a minute!"

"What?"

"This ain't 'bout *The Road Warrior* at all," cried Laurel, arms akimbo, "this is about that boy—Dashawn!"

"What if it is?" cried Sha'Tanya, getting in Laurel's face.

"Girl, I would slap you so hard," started Laurel, angrily, "you would run straight to school!"

"That's funny," said Sha'Tanya, with a chuckle,

"you should do comedy."

"I ain't laughing," cried Laurel, with a stern look, "I told you he's bad news!"

"Why," Sha'Tanya replied, throwing her hands in the air, "because he goes to school in South Sea Village?"

"Because he's a womanizer," cried Laurel, folding her arms, "and yes—'Dead Sea' children are trouble!"

Suddenly, Sha'Tanya held out her hand, signalling Laurel to stop, as she shushed her.

"You hear that?"

"What?"

"The bald-patched green monkey, calling for one of the park custodians," cried Sha'Tanya, in a panic, "he's getting a woman to come in here for us; I gotta get out of here!"

Sha'Tanya started to walk towards the door, but Laurel gripped her by the shoulder and halted her from behind.

"What exactly do you plan to do?" asked Laurel.

"Make a run for it," replied Sha'Tanya, staring intently through the door, determined to get her seat and meet Dashawn.

"If this is so important to you," said Laurel, with a sigh, "the least I can do is give you a fighting chance."

Sha'Tanya turned around to see Laurel pointing at the small window at the end of the corridor. There were more than a few questions in her head, but she knew that a park custodian could be upon them at any moment, so she didn't ask any questions, just followed Laurel's lead.

THE SEAT

With no time to waste, Laurel climbed up onto the counter, then extended her hand to Sha'Tanya, helping her up onto the counter with a mighty pull. Not only was Laurel big, she was extremely strong for her age and she proceeded to put that strength to good use.

Laurel took Sha'Tanya's backpack and rested it by one of the sinks on the counter. Then, getting behind Sha'Tanya, Laurel hugged her torso from behind tightly, and lifted, hoisting Sha'Tanya's body up off the counter enough for her to wedge her feet against the back wall of the bathroom. With her feet against the wall, and Laurel holding her in place, Sha'Tanya then walked up the wall at a slight angle until her feet reached the small window.

Sha'Tanya then placed her feet just inside of the window sill, as Laurel lifted and pushed her, while stepping forward, sending her feetfirst through the window. When she was far enough through the window, she used her hands to grip the top of the window frame.

"Don't worry 'bout me," Laurel whispered as she released Sha'Tanya, allowing her to guide the rest of her body through the window, "go, get your seat—but don't say I didn't warn you."

Eventually, the only part of Sha'Tanya inside the bathroom was her hands, which kept a grip on the window frame. She finally released the window frame, allowing herself to fall to the ground outside, landing in a crouch.

Now, outside the bathroom, Sha'Tanya turned around to face the window which she had just come through, and caught her backpack, which Laurel threw through the window. Sha'Tanya paused for a moment, thinking about the sacrifice Laurel was making for her, even though she didn't approve of her motivation to meet Dashawn. That moment was brief, however, as Sha'Tanya started to hear some commotion on the other side of the bathroom and took off running like the wind in a hurricane. She identified the nearest gap in the nearest hedge and dashed through it.

Finally, liberated from the park, there was no time to calm herself; she trotted with pace along the sidewalk of the busy road on the other side of the hedge, trying to get to a bus stop in time.

Suddenly, a bus came barrelling around a corner in the distance. Like *Turbulence*, it was adorned with spoilers, decorative roof racks, side skirts and decorative window tints. The edge of the front windscreen tint carried lettering, spelling out the words "Road Warrior".

Sha'Tanya's heart pounded with force as she extended her hand to stop the bus, while still very far from a bus stop. As the bus approached, a short, dark conductor, with a gold tooth and three gold chains around his neck, leaned through the door and called out to her.

"Run and jump, 'Sweetness'!" he shouted in a rough voice.

Sha'Tanya wasted no time; she started running as the driver slowed down just enough to roughly match her pace. Then, with a racing heart, she jumped through the door of the still moving vehicle. As her foot hit the step, the driver immediately increased speed, without ever stopping. The conductor gripped her firmly to ensure she didn't fall out, and the driver closed the door behind her. She had seen many people attempt this stunt, with disastrous results, and she was relieved that she had nailed her performance.

Sha'Tanya didn't wait for her heartrate to decrease; she immediately made her way through the crowded bus, to stand closer to the back. This time, she wasn't so fortunate as to receive a seat before reaching the bus yard, but the door remained intact and that was good enough for Sha'Tanya.

Minutes later, the bus reached the bus yard. As it barrelled around a corner, heading into the main boarding area, the driver pressed the musical air horn, signalling the arrival of *The Road Warrior*.

"'Dead Sea' with seats and moving!" shouted the conductor, hanging through the door as the bus cleared the corner and prepared to stop.

By the time the bus came to a complete stop, a stampede of children descended upon it from all corners of the bus yard. The disembarking passengers promptly vacated their seats and prepared themselves to battle against the invading army, who were bound for South Sea Village. The ensuing battle between embarking and disembarking passengers provided Sha'Tanya with the opportunity she sought for the entire morning—choosing her seat. A couple of older boys climbed through windows, but by this time, Sha'Tanya had already taken up position in the left corner of the back seat.

Sha'Tanya savoured the moment, as she sat in the black and red, upholstered seat, surrounded by red window tint and airbrushed artwork of checkered flags. There were blood splashes airbrushed over the checkered flags.

"It's fitting I should be surrounded by blood splashed checkered flags," Sha'Tanya thought to herself, as the bus was inundated, "I've been racing and battling for this seat the entire morning."

In short order, the bus was full of South Sea Secondary students, and even some of Sha'Tanya's schoolmates who had also opted to take *The Road Warrior* in the absence of *Turbulence*. As the driver revved the engine to start a new journey, Sha'Tanya anxiously tried to look through the crowd, hoping to see Dashawn.

Suddenly, a dark, well-toned boy burst through the crowd to stand in the very back of the bus. Sha'Tanya's heart skipped a beat when she saw this Greek sculpture in the making. It skipped another when he made eye contact with her, and yet, another, when he spoke.

"Sha'Tanya," he cried, with a beaming smile, "I didn't think I would see you today; *Turbulence* went off the road and the truancy officers seem to be out in full force."

"It was a battle," replied Sha'Tanya with a sigh, "Laurel sacrificed herself to a monkey-looking truancy officer so that I could get this seat."

"She's a good friend," replied Dashawn, nodding his head in approval, as the driver started to move forward, "but yeah, this morning was rough; I ain't even get my usual backseat."

Sha'Tanya was hoping to sit next to Dashawn on the ride but she saw this as an opportunity to be even closer to her partially-chiselled Greek sculpture.

"You wanna sit down?" she asked quickly, before the bus properly took off.

Dashawn wasted no time in accepting the offer, taking Sha'Tanya's seat as she made a new seat—on Dashawn's lap.

In short order, loud music started blasting and the bus jolted forward. The driver held the first gear as he moved through the bus yard, like a hunter pulling on a slingshot before releasing a projectile. The children cheered and hit the sides of the bus in anticipation of the inevitable release, Sha'Tanya and Dashawn included. Finally, the driver started changing the gears and bolted out of the bus yard like a plane on a runway.

To exit the bus yard, the buses took a long, deserted road, about three hundred metres long, with a big bend in the middle. To the right of the road were marshes and a mossy canal, separated from the road by a high footpath. From Sha'Tanya's viewpoint, on the left side of the bus, there was only gravel and patches of grass.

As the bus sped along this road, the children instigated the driver to execute reckless manoeuvres.

"Lean it like you mean it!" chanted the children, as the bus approached the bend in the road.

The driver made a wide swerve before banking into the bend, causing the bus to lean to the right. Dashawn held the handle bar on the back of the seat in front of him, bracing Sha'Tanya's body from toppling over to the right. As the children cheered in approval of the driver's antics, Sha'Tanya joined them, but her cheers were in approval of Dashawn's chiselled biceps, against which she was braced. Through the window, she could see three buses at the end of the road, waiting to turn onto the main road, along which the public park was set. As the bus cleared the bend and exited its lean, to Sha'Tanya's shock, it didn't show any signs of reducing speed, despite the wide, single-lane road being blocked by a line of three stationary buses.

"This driver's head screwed on backwards!" cried Sha'Tanya, in shock and a little horror, as the driver sharply banked off the last bus in the line.

The Road Warrior then proceeded to live up to its name, narrowly squeezing through the space between the other buses and the high footpath, and speeding past the three outgoing buses to reach the junction to the main road in short order. Once there, the driver pushed the front of the bus onto the main road, forcing oncoming cars to brake suddenly. *The Road Warrior* then barrelled onto the main road fully, and continued its rough, rapid journey before meeting traffic and being forced to stop.

"You gotta admit," said Dashawn, "this is a rougher ride than *Turbulence*."

"How come you ride *Turbulence*, then," Sha'Tanya asked, looking back into his face with a quizzical look.

"Because," started Dashawn, in a smooth voice as he gazed into her eyes, "you ride *Turbulence*, and I ain't meet a South Sea girl yet that can touch you—positively stunning."

Sha'Tanya tried to contain an inward explosion of emotions. She struggled to bring her thoughts and feelings into subjection, so she could determine the right response.

On the one hand, she was thoroughly flattered by Dashawn's comment—and she did, in fact, believe that she was superior to all the 'Dead Sea' girls combined.

On the other hand, Laurel's words were still faintly echoing around her mind.

"He's a womanizer … 'Dead Sea' children are trouble!"

Before she could settle her thoughts, the driver revved the engine and dashed through a minor road on the right. Sha'Tanya looked at Dashawn in utter astonishment before turning around to ascertain what the driver was trying to accomplish, as the bus raced along the hedges of the public park.

Suddenly, the bus swerved to the right, before sharply banking to the left, into the driveway of the public park. Dashawn braced Sha'Tanya's body again, as the bus leaned sharply into the turn. Finally, the bus returned to an upright position—but not for long. Sha'Tanya sat in astonishment as the driver proceeded to skilfully rock the bus from side to side, right through the public park.

"Shake it till you break it!" chanted the children in an eruption of excitement.

"This is one morning I ain't ever gonna forget," said Dashawn, as he gripped the handlebar with both arms, one on either side of Sha'Tanya, keeping her steady as the bus rocked.

"Because of the 'shakes'?" asked Sha'Tanya, with anxiety burning in her gut.

"Because of the queen I get to enjoy them with,"

replied Dashawn, in a voice smoother than a wet balloon.

Sha'Tanya blushed and a wide smile invaded her face as the 'shakes' continued.

Finally, the bus barrelled out of the park through another opening, and back onto the main road. Cutting through the park had taken them around the traffic congestion and they were now speeding along the main road approaching the hospital.

As they approached the hospital, Sha'Tanya remembered stepping out of the car earlier that morning, meeting Laurel, and all the events that followed. In that moment, she beamed with triumph. She had set out to get a seat in a popular bus, and to interface with Dashawn; despite many challenges, and warnings, she had remained strong-willed and managed to attain her heart's desires in the end.

Suddenly, her thoughts were interrupted by a wailing siren and she looked through the back windscreen to see a police officer's bike approaching. The music stopped abruptly and the bus came to a halt, as did the officer, who promptly dismounted.

"Where do these 'motorbycle' policemen come from?" thought Sha'Tanya, annoyed as she looked through the window.

She watched with interest as the conductor stepped onto the sidewalk to meet the tall, slender officer, who removed their helmet to reveal their face to the conductor; it was a dark woman, with short curls.

"This bus is only supposed to carry seven standing passengers!" shouted the officer. "I hope you ain't collect bus fare yet, 'cause those children gotta get out of there!"

The officer started to survey the passengers from outside the bus, as if she were trying to ascertain the number of children inside before removing them.

"I can't even see through this …" started the officer before making eye contact with Sha'Tanya.

"Wait a minute! I can't believe what I'm seeing!" cried the officer, with her arms akimbo and a stern face. "You can't be older than thirteen, and sitting in a boy's lap; get out of that bus, now!"

Sha'Tanya gripped her backpack and made her way through the crowd in utter bewilderment. There was a tornado of emotions raging inside of her—fear, disappointment, humiliation, sadness and anger. As she disembarked the bus, she couldn't even distinguish between the different emotions; she just knew that she felt really bad, and she struggled to keep the reservoir in her eyes from rupturing. The seat she had fought for the entire morning, was her very undoing. In that moment, she was haunted by Laurel's words, echoing in her mind.

"Go, get your seat—but don't say I didn't warn you."

To add insult to injury, her undoing was very public. She made her way from the bus to the officer's side, looking down at the sidewalk the entire time. In that moment, she could feel everyone's eyes on her but she couldn't bring herself to make eye contact with any-one—especially Dashawn.

The officer was seemingly so disturbed by the sight

of Sha'Tanya on Dashawn's lap that she allowed the bus to continue without removing anyone else. As Sha'Tanya heard the bus drive off, she could keep the tears sequestered no more, and allowed them to flow freely down her cheeks.

Just then, she felt an arm around her shoulder, and heard the voice of the officer softly in her ear.

"I was once you, so I know that what I'm about to say isn't going to bear fruit today, or tomorrow," she said, "but some day in the near future, I want you to remember my words today."

Sha'Tanya just listened, still with her head down and her eyes closed.

"There's more to life than boys and reckless fun," continued the officer, "and there's more to you than that; you are better than this, you just have to realise it!"

Suddenly, she heard the sound of an engine and a familiar voice pierced her ears.

"Can I be of assistance, officer?"

Sha'Tanya opened her eyes to the most horrible sight she could have imagined—the bald-patched green monkey, driving the white truant van.

The truancy officer made direct eye contact with Sha'Tanya, and uttered the worst words she could have imagined.

"I have a seat just for you!"

ERROR!

Sha'Tanya hurried along a quiet residential road with her gel slicked hair shining and her tightly girded stomach ablaze with anxiety. As she zoomed past nicely painted houses, she could see the object of her anxiety in the distance, at the end of the road—her school.

Sha'Tanya exited the residential road onto an adjoining road, which ran along the back wall of her school. She crossed the road and hurried along the school wall with building anxiety and a little fear. These emotions only ballooned as she reached the back gate of the school, to find it had already been closed.

"This is bad," she thought, as she peered through the gate, briefly making eye contact with a female prefect, who stared at her with a disapproving expression.

She wasted no time in making her way around the compound, to the front entrance of the school—a journey which seemed to take an eternity. She considered climbing over one of the lower sections of the wall, but didn't think she could make it while carrying her backpack. Finally, she arrived at the front gate, and braced herself for what awaited her.

"If I get another late slip, I'm finished," she thought, as she hurried through the gate and up a worn driveway, paranoidly scanning for authority figures like an animal scanning for predators.

To her shock, she reached the office without encountering a guard, groundsman or teacher.

"I ain't complaining," she thought to herself, as she hurried past the office, "but I wonder how I managed to get this far without getting into trouble."

She hurriedly entered a long walkway, set between hedges and under a trellis, leading to the school hall. Not long into her trek up this walkway, a slim, dark, first-form boy dashed past her.

"Excuse me," he cried, as he zoomed past her.

Before she could process this, a huge, brown woman, brandishing a belt, came barrelling after him, almost knocking into her.

"Get out of the way, little girl," shouted the woman.

"Who you calling 'little girl'?" Sha'Tanya shouted in reply, thinking how much shapelier and more attractive she was than the woman. "Error!"

Her focus quickly changed, however, as she noticed the uproar this woman and the boy she was chasing had apparently caused within the school. Two teachers and a guard zoomed past her in short order, showing no interest in her tardiness. The student body was mobilised, in a frenzy of chatter and laughter. Though highly curious about what was transpiring, relief overshadowed curiosity, and she made a dash for the nearest group of students, intent to blend into the crowd. The crowd's focus was on the situation at hand but Sha'Tanya's focus was on her own situation. She dashed through the crowds of students, to deposit her backpack in her classroom—which was close to the hall—and then made her way back down to the office block, to freshen up in the bathroom.

Once in the bathroom, her anxiety succumbed to peace, and she breathed a sigh of relief as she stood over a sink, in front of a mirror, seeking to make herself as fresh as possible.

"Sha'Tanya?" came a voice from the nearby bathroom entrance.

Sha'Tanya looked around to see a tall, thick, dark girl with corn rows—her friend, Laurel.

"I thought it was you," said Laurel, walking into the bathroom and leaning against the blank wall behind the sinks. "What happened that you just got to school?"

"Girl, I just went through stress," replied Sha'Tanya, shaking her head as she looked at Laurel via her reflection in the mirror.

"Trouble with truancy officers?"

"No, girl," cried Sha'Tanya, turning around to face Laurel, "I' just come from 'The Dead Sea'."

"Your head screwed on backwards?" asked Laurel, with her arms akimbo. "You have any idea how dangerous that area is?"

"Relax yourself," said Sha'Tanya, softly, as she held both of her hands out towards Laurel, "people go to school in that area."

"The bus drops them by the school," replied Laurel, sternly, "they don't have to walk through the area."

"Underneath all the drugs and deviance, it's just a village—South Sea Village."

"That village is known as 'The Dead Sea' for a reason," continued Laurel, passionately, "you could have gone missing!"

"This girl really thinks somebody could capture and keep contained, the dynamite which is Sha'Tanya Carter?" thought Sha'Tanya, as she gave Laurel a critical stare, before verbalising the thought in a single word.

"Error!"

Suddenly, their conversation was interrupted by the flush of a toilet.

"Oh, shoot; who now flush that 'tylit'?" whispered Sha'Tanya, as the girls turned to peer deeper into the bathroom, into the midsection, which featured eight toilet stalls. "I ain't need people in my business today."

A tall, bony, fair skinned girl with a shoulder length ponytail exited one of the stalls with a backpack in hand, and proceeded to one of the sinks; it was Emelia Harris, a classmate with whom Sha'Tanya shared a mutual dislike.

"I thought your uniform was tight because it was the same one from last year," started Emelia, cutting her eyes at Sha'Tanya as she proceeded to wash her hands at the adjacent sink, "but now, I see you're trying to fit in with the lowlife, lower-class 'Dead Sea' girls."

"My uniform fits this way because I have the shape

to fill it out," quipped Sha'Tanya, promptly, "yours would fit better if you weren't as flat as an ironing board."

Emelia stepped towards Sha'Tanya with a threatening demeaner, but as quickly as she had stepped, Laurel inserted her arm between the two girls, and stood staring at Emelia with a cruel expression.

"Oh, I'm sorry," said Sha'Tanya, pretending to casually examine her nails, "you were about to do something?"

Emelia gave Sha'Tanya a look colder than a fresh snow cone, and exited the bathroom as Sha'Tanya laughed heartily. Sha'Tanya exited the bathroom shortly after, never finishing her conversation with Laurel. The morning's commotion had gone well into the first period; she didn't know how soon the school would be brought into order but she thought it prudent to prepare for a math test, which was coming soon in the second period.

A little later that morning, just as the second period was about to commence, Sha'Tanya was in her class, doing last-minute prep for the impending test. The classroom consisted of seven rows of four desks, with the teacher's desk at the top, in the opposite corner from the door. Sha'Tanya sat at the first desk in the back row, on the same side as the door, next to Laurel. A short, brown, medium height, medium build girl with her hair gelled into a bun, approached her in a frenzy; it was her friend, Lystra.

"Listen 'Tan Tan'," cried the girl, "I just overheard some girls saying that Dashawn carried you to make out in the 'The Dead Sea' this morning."

Sha'Tanya's world went dark. All the mathematics she had studied evacuated her mind in that moment. All she could think about was the perception these girls had of her, and the audacity they had, to make such an assertion. These thoughts were passionately summarised into a single outburst.

"Error!"

At that moment, a short, dark man, with thick eyebrows and a bald patch, entered the classroom with a long wooden rule, as though it were a walking stick; it was Mr. Warner, the teacher for that period.

Sha'Tanya put her books away and took her scientific calculator out of her backpack, placing it on the desk with a pensive look on her face. As she looked at the calculator on the desk, a bevy of emotions raced around the track, which was her heart; a moment ago, she was prepped and filled with zeal to ace this test, but now, she was deflated and filled with shame, anger and dread.

The test did not go well for Sha'Tanya; all she could focus on was the rumour being spread. She pondered the identities of the girls Lystra had overheard. She also pondered who could have started such a vicious rumour. By the end of the period, she had reached a conclusion on the latter question.

As the teacher exited the class with the test papers, and the students rose to head over to the science lab for their next period, Sha'Tanya signalled to Laurel to walk close to her.

"Girl, that test just manhandled me," said Laurel,

as she joined Sha'Tanya.

"Forget that; this time, Emelia Harris has gone too far," said Sha'Tanya, as the girls made their way out of the class.

"That was rude!" cried Laurel, before grabbing her chin with a ponderous look. "You sure it was Emelia?"

"This morning, she was listening when I told you I was in 'The Dead Sea'—pretending to use a 'tylit'," started Sha'Tanya, as the girls made their way past the hall, "who else could've spread this?"

"You sure she was pretending to use the toilet?" asked Laurel, with a chuckle.

"She was probably in there with a notebook, taking notes; who carries a backpack to the toilet?" cried Sha'Tanya, as they made their way through the school. "I know she's the culprit and I want you to beat the sponge out of that little ironing board."

"Hold up! People call me your bodyguard, and that's fine," said Laurel, raising her hands in a defensive posture, "I ain't gonna let anybody lay a hand on you, but at the same time, I ain't gonna be your thug for hire—no way!"

"So, she gets to drag my name through the mud with a nasty rumour?" cried Sha'Tanya, blocking Laurel's path on the hardcourt in the middle of the school.

"Is it really a rumour?" asked Laurel, pausing and staring at Sha'Tanya intently with her arms folded.

"I can't believe you're actually standing up here asking me that question," cried an offended Sha'Tanya, with her arms akimbo.

"You told me not to look for you this morning 'cause you're taking the early trip; then you revealed that you went to 'The Dead Sea'," started Laurel, giving Sha'Tanya a critical stare. "You expect me to believe that you weren't with Dashawn?"

"Yes, I was with Dashawn," cried Sha'Tanya, getting into Laurel's face, "but you ain't understand what went down!"

"I understand that you want me to beat somebody for saying something that is at least two thirds true," cried Laurel, pushing past Sha'Tanya and continuing across the hardcourt to the science lab, "she couldn't say those things if you weren't running 'bout behind a South Sea womanizer like Dashawn."

Sha'Tanya's heart sank in that moment.

"If my own best friend believes the rumour," she thought, "everyone else in the school will, too."

Sha'Tanya just stood and watched Laurel walk away, with a bevy of emotions colliding inside of her like balls in a lottery machine. She was frustrated with herself for getting to school late, angry with Emelia for starting the rumour, disappointed in Laurel for believing it, and for not beating Emelia. Frustration, disappointment, anger—which emotion would come out on top? Finally, the lottery draw concluded; anger was the winning emotion, and that anger was directed towards Emelia.

Finally, Sha'Tanya stormed off across the hardcourt—but not towards the science lab. She made her way to a secluded, concreted area at the back of the school. There was a garbage skip, an emergency water tank, and a non-operational kiln with the school wall providing a backdrop. She entered the area to find a group of boys scrambling for cover.

"Relax, men," she said, posing with one arm akimbo, "look at this shiny hair; I ain't Principal Harding."

An extremely dark boy, with a hippopotamus nose, pinkish eyes and thick shrubbery for hair stepped forward. This was Ricardo, the school bully; he was a fourth-former who was big for his age and not to be messed with.

"Who told you 'bout the boys' gambling spot, Sha'Tanya?" asked Ricardo, with his arms folded.

"Boy, please," started Sha'Tanya, with attitude, "I am Sha'Tanya Carter; I know some of everything that goes on 'bout here."

"Sorry, we don't gamble with girls," said Ricardo, turning to walk away.

"This boy thinks I'm looking to throw away what little money I have, in a game of chance?" Sha'Tanya thought to herself, before encapsulating the thought in a single, bite-sized word.

"Error!" cried Sha'Tanya. "I ain't here to gamble; I'm looking to do business with you. I need somebody that can't be traced back to me."

Ricardo paused, and turned around to face Sha'Tanya with an intrigued look on his face.

"You got my attention," he said, before leading Sha'Tanya over to the kiln to discuss the matter privately.

"Sha'Tanya Carter gets what she wants," Sha'Tanya thought, as she followed Ricardo to the kiln. "Emelia

Harris is going down—and that so-called friend, Laurel is going to do it, even if it takes her down too!"

About thirty-five minutes later, a plan was in motion. The period ended and Sha'Tanya's classmates where once again traversing across the hardcourt, this time on their way back to the classroom. Sha'Tanya watched from a distance as Ricardo approached Emelia and engaged her in conversation. She smiled widely when she saw Emelia's facial expression go from scepticism to intrigue; she appeared to be taking the bait.

"It's only a matter of time now," Sha'Tanya thought, as she made her way back to the classroom, smiling ear to ear. Little did she know, that smile was about to change.

She had reached the hall when she heard footsteps running behind her, and a familiar voice calling her name. She stopped and turned around to see Laurel running after her.

"I can't believe you skipped class!" cried Laurel, embracing her with a tight hug upon her arrival. "Look, I'm sorry I believed a rumour over my best friend; give me your side of the story at lunchtime."

Sha'Tanya was paralysed with shock; In that moment, she realised that she had made a grave error. She didn't know how to respond to Laurel's unexpected change of heart—especially after the plan she and Ricardo had set in motion. Fortunately, there was no time for her to render a response, even if she had one, as the teacher for that period arrived.

"Break it up," cried a thick, dark, rough-looking man with grey stubble, "this is second form, not day care, and I'm a history teacher, not a guidance counsellor!"

"Yes, Mr. Greenidge," cried Laurel, breaking her embrace at once and following the teacher to the classroom.

Sha'Tanya followed like a zombie; her entire world went dark as she tried to come to terms with the implications of what she had just set in motion. For that period, Mr. Greenidge dealt with the implications of the second world war on the Caribbean. Sha'Tanya couldn't focus on the world war, however, as she was too preoccupied with the local "girl war" to come.

Finally, the bell rang, signalling recess. As her classmates rejoiced, the sound of the bell filled Sha'Tanya with dread, like a civil defence siren in a war zone, signalling the possibility of explosive conditions at any moment. As she followed Laurel out of the classroom, she was filled with anxiety, as if walking out onto a live battlefield. As they approached the hall, she remained very alert, with the nerve-racking expectation that a bomb—of her making—could go off at any moment.

"Well," said Laurel, as they passed the hall, "you gonna tell me what really happened or not?"

"Look, I lent Dashawn my scientific calculator until today," started Sha'Tanya. "The boy had the nerve to call me and tell me that I can't get it back for this morning, 'cause he left it in his desk at school."

By this time, the girls were approaching the canteen; Sha'Tanya tried to get out as much of her explanation as possible before they reached the canteen.

"When he told me that, I was like, 'Error! I got a

test in the morning'," she continued, speaking more quickly than before, "so he agreed to meet me for the early trip, so that I could go to South Sea Secondary, get what is mine, and get my behind here before assembly."

"Oh," cried Laurel, with a shocked expression, as the girls reached the canteen and scanned it for a queue to join.

"Some hungry-looking South Sea girls, intimidated by my awesomeness, tried to start a fight," said Sha'Tanya, raising her hands in a defensive posture, as Laurel stopped and opened her mouth in shock. "I told them I wasn't there to fight over anybody, got what was mine, and got out of there."

"Wise choice," said Laurel, with a chuckle, "you couldn't fight a turtle."

"I don't need to; I have you for that," Sha'Tanya replied, cutting her eyes at Laurel. "Anyway, Dashawn showed me all the shortcuts, but I still got here late."

"It's a good thing the school was in an uproar," said Laurel, with a chuckle, as they proceeded to join a queue, "some boy's mother came down here to flog him."

"I'm so sorry I missed that action!" cried Sha'Tanya, bursting out in laughter, forgetting about any impending explosion for a moment.

Suddenly, Lystra came running up to them in a frenzy, sending alarms off in Sha'Tanya's head.

"Laurel, Laurel, Laurel," cried Lystra, as Sha'Tanya's heart pounded with apprehension, "Emelia Harris going 'bout telling people that your father got locked up

ERROR!

for stealing a tin of sardines!"

In that moment, it was as if time froze for Sha'Tanya. She could see Laurel's facial expression changing from quizzical to livid, and she could see Lystra's facial expression changing from concerned to alarmed—an expression Sha'Tanya shared.

Laurel was big for her age and remarkably strong, but she was also very level-headed and difficult to provoke. When she was provoked, however, it could be very dangerous; that much strength under the command of a hot head could lead to disastrous results. Sha'Tanya knew this very well, and she was the only person in the school who understood just how sensitive Laurel would be to this particular rumour.

Laurel charged out of the canteen like a missile. The moment Sha'Tanya had been dreading was upon her; the missile had been fired and an explosion was imminent. An hour ago, Sha'Tanya had been counting on this explosion, but now, after Laurel had proven herself to be a truly remarkable friend, she wanted nothing more than a ceasefire. Normally, she was the first to run to safety, but on this occasion, she thrust herself into the conflict, and took off behind Laurel, beckoning to Lystra to join her.

"Be cool, Laurel!" cried Sha'Tanya, grabbing Laurel's arm.

"Don't tell me to be cool," cried Laurel, shaking loose of Sha'Tanya's grip, "I'm gonna hit that malicious ironing board so hard, she will grow a shape!"

"You can't do this in the middle of recess," cried Lystra, as Laurel continued to storm through the school in search of Emelia, "you could get flogged, maybe even suspended!"

"I ain't care," cried Laurel, passionately, "she ain't know where I came from; what it is to be hungry till your navel touching your back, and your father struggling to keep you alive!"

Sha'Tanya started to panic inside; it seemed impossible to halt this attack. She tried to think of the correct abort codes for the missile; what could she possibly say to pacify Laurel?

Just then, Sha'Tanya froze in her tracks, grabbing Lystra's hand as she saw Emelia sitting on a bench, eating her lunch. She made eye contact with Lystra as Laurel charged towards Emelia, screaming her name; the missile was target-locked.

"Emelia Harris!" screamed Laurel as she zeroed in on her target.

Emelia looked around, saw Laurel charging in, dropped her lunch and took off running. Sha'Tanya and Lystra ran behind them, like cameramen chasing the action in a National Geographic documentary—a mighty lioness chasing an anorexic antelope.

As the chase continued through the school, many excited spectators began to follow the girls, like tourists on a safari hoping for a glimpse of wildlife action.

"Emelia can't keep this up; Laurel has more stamina than a pack of sleigh dogs," Sha'Tanya thought, as the gap between the girls started to narrow. "I ain't know what to do when she catches this girl."

Emelia seemingly made the same assessment Sha'Tanya did, as she dashed across the hardcourt in the middle of the school and into a classroom, with Laurel hot on her heels, followed by Sha'Tanya, Lystra and a throng of roaring students.

Once in the classroom, Emelia dashed behind a desk, grabbed a chair and turned around to face Laurel, who had just come through the door.

"Stand back!" cried Emelia, holding the chair in front of her, pointing its legs at Laurel, with the desk between them.

Sha'Tanya entered the classroom behind Laurel, grabbing her by the arm from behind.

"She ain't worth it, Laurel," she cried, in a last-ditch effort to deescalate the situation before Laurel got into serious trouble.

Laurel pulled her arm out of Sha'Tanya's grasp, grabbed the desk by one of its legs, and with a single volley, threw it across the entire length of the classroom, as the crowd peered through the windows, cheering. Sha'Tanya quickly re-evaluated her position, taking her own advice—Emelia wasn't worth it.

"I ain't taking a stray blow for that ironing board," Sha'Tanya thought, as she scampered under a desk. "Error!"

Sha'Tanya resolved that she couldn't save Laurel from punishment; the least she could do now was enjoy Emelia's beating from a fortified position.

Emelia lunged forward, swinging the chair at Laurel, who caught it by a leg, with one hand. Laurel proceeded to rip the chair out of Emelia's grasp and throw it across the classroom. The chair hit the desk under which Sha'Tanya had taken cover, sending her scampering from under it.

As Sha'Tanya took cover under another desk, Laurel advanced and gave Emelia a backhand slap across her face. Emelia went flying to the right, as her ponytail, now detached, went flying to the left, much to the amusement of Sha'Tanya and the crowd.

Suddenly, a stern voice pierced Sha'Tanya's ears, immediately inducing silence in the crowd.

"Cease and settle!"

It was Principal Harding, a tall, clear man with an Adam's apple like a golf ball, and a hairline receding like a runaway rumour; there was no getting it back.

Sha'Tanya watched from under the desk as the principal charged into the classroom with a huge tamarind rod, known in student circles as "*The Enemy*", and addressed the warring girls.

"A mother invades the school with a belt, and now this; what is going on in this school today?" cried Mr. Harding, surveying the state of the classroom. "You know we have a zero-tolerance policy on fighting; assume the position!"

Emelia began to cry immediately, as the girls stood at attention and awaited the rod. Laurel was flogged first. Sha'Tanya couldn't bring herself to watch the flogging, but her heart was pierced with the sound of each lash. Laurel had proven to be a better friend to her, than she was to Laurel. In that moment, she was ashamed of herself for plotting Emelia's demise at Laurel's expense, but what was done was done.

Eventually, Emelia's turn came, lifting Sha'Tanya's spirits.

"Now you!" came Mr. Harding's voice.

Sha'Tanya made sure her eyes were open for this flogging. As the lashes commenced, she had to cover her mouth, fighting to contain her laughter as Emelia howled and contorted with every lash. She found it poetically fitting that *The Enemy* should be the instrument of torment for her enemy.

"That's what happens when you spread rumours 'bout Sha'Tanya Carter," she thought. "When you mess with dynamite, you might just get blown up!"

The principal concluded his deed and sent the girls out of the room, before exiting himself. When the dust had settled, Sha'Tanya retrieved Emelia's fake ponytail from the floor, and exited the class, making her way towards the canteen. She threaded across the hardcourt, looking at the hairpiece, and plotting how she could use it to best humiliate Emelia.

"Maybe it wasn't that big of an error after all," she started to reassure herself, "Emelia needed to be dealt with and Laurel's a big girl; she can take the lashes, and she wasn't suspended."

Suddenly, she heard someone call out her name and turned around to see Ricardo running towards her.

"I gave Emelia the info, she couldn't keep it to herself and you got what you wanted," he said, with his arms folded, upon reaching her, "you had better keep your end of the bargain."

"Don't worry, I'll pay your bus fare for a week," said Sha'Tanya, staring into his pinkish eyes, thinking she had negotiated a good deal; both she and Ricardo faithfully rode a specific bus, called *Turbulence*, and she had enough favour with the conductor to ride free for a few days.

"Oh, and just for your information," said Ricardo, as they were about to part ways, "it ain't Emelia that started the rumour 'bout you."

"What?" cried Sha'Tanya, staring at Ricardo with shock and alarm.

"It was a prefect … girl named Izzy," said Ricardo, with a smug look, "she saw you getting in *Turbulence* on the early trip …"

"Then she saw me through the gate, coming from the direction of South Sea Village," said Sha'Tanya, finishing the narrative as she remembered seeing the prefect earlier that morning at the back gate.

"Just thought you would like to know," said Ricardo, walking away, "but a deal is a deal."

Sha'Tanya felt horrible as she stood there, holding the ponytail and processing what had just happened. She had said the word "error" many times already for that day—each time, directed at someone else—but this time, she was the one in error. Two people had been flogged because of her misguided wrath. One of those people was her best friend, who also had sensitive, personal information leaked to the student body, because of her misplaced anger. As she stood there, frozen in place, these thoughts were verbalised in one, softly whispered word.

"Error."

ENDGAME

Sha'Tanya sat on her couch in total shambles, weeping bitterly. She felt stupid and ashamed, and she was scared to even imagine how much worse her situation could have been. As she sat there, wishing she had taken a different path, the events of that day flashed before her mind's eye like a movie.

Earlier that morning, she had risen from her slumber well before sunrise—something which almost never happened. She was bursting with excitement from the time her eyes popped open. Ten minutes later, she had showered, and five minutes after that, she had pressed a tight, red top and a short, purple pants. Within another five minutes, she had applied lotion to her skin, dressed, glossed her lips, powdered her neck and emptied a tub of hair gel on her hair.

In short order, she was out of her cosy bedroom and banging on the door of her mother's adjacent bedroom. A slim, dark, groggy-looking woman in a burgundy night gown with red, frizzy hair, opened the door.

"Why you ain't sleeping?" asked the woman, with one arm akimbo. "If there was school today, you wouldn't be up yet."

"Don't be like that, Mum," replied Sha'Tanya, with her arms folded, "I left home extra-early a day last week."

"You had a test; that wasn't a typical school day for you," said her mother, leaning lazily against the door-post. "Now, it's Teacher's Professional Day, Laurel is supposed to be coming over and you're banging down my door at this time, fully dressed already; I should've sent you to your father's house for the day."

"This woman seems to think I am a little girl; does she know that I'm thirteen, and shaving my arm pits?" thought Sha'Tanya, before verbally responding.

"Error" she cried, "I am a big girl, I don't need a babysitter!"

"Why are you at my door?" asked her mother, with an exasperated look.

"Breakfast would be nice," started Sha'Tanya, while examining her nails, "and I need extra money to solve a crisis; my hair gel is gone."

"Error! You're a 'big girl'; you can solve your hair crisis out of whatever money you have saved," said her mother, leaving the door and heading back to her bed.

"What about breakfast?" cried Sha'Tanya, folding her arms with a pout.

"I have unfinished business with my bed," came her mother's voice, "you can feed yourself, 'big girl'; don't burn down my house!"

Sha'Tanya cut her eyes and marched off through

the cream, wooden walls, to the kitchen. She was upset that she had been left to her own devices for breakfast, but simultaneously elated at the prospect of being left to her own devices for the rest of the day.

If only she could have known how that day would turn out, she could have saved herself a lot of heartache. Unfortunately, there was no prophetic vision to be had, and no warnings of danger—yet.

An hour later, Sha'Tanya was in town, standing on a sidewalk, in the bus yard. Behind her were various vendors operating out of wooden kiosks. In front of her was a huge asphalt area where the buses stopped for passengers to disembark, before proceeding to their prescribed loading points. After a short wait, a bus came around the corner, into the bus yard, and stopped by the spot where Sha'Tanya stood. In short order, a tall, thick, dark girl with corn rows disembarked the bus, wearing long denim pants, and a yellow t-shirt.

"Really, Laurel?" cried Sha'Tanya, standing with one arm akimbo and giving her friend a critical look.

"What," asked Laurel, with a concerned look, "am I late?"

"No, you're right on time," said Sha'Tanya, maintaining her look and posture, "but you actually came to town in this plain, rust-bucket bus."

"I like a nice-looking bus too," cried Laurel, cutting her eyes at Sha'Tanya, "but I was trying to be on time."

"Girl, you put punctuality ahead of style?" cried Sha'Tanya, with a repulsed expression, as the girls started walking to a more shaded spot. "Error!"

"Girl, if I didn't like you so much," started Laurel, with her arms akimbo, "I would slap you so hard, the gel would separate from your hair!"

Sha'Tanya held over in a hearty laugh.

"You better be appreciative," said Laurel, folding her arms and giving Sha'Tanya a stern look, "you got me spending my off-day on bodyguard duty."

"Wait, hold up …" cried Sha'Tanya, holding up her index finder, "you decided you needed to guard me; I ain't need protection."

"You plan to be home alone, with your new, fourteen-year-old boyfriend, and your mother ain't know 'bout it," cried Laurel, staring intently at Sha'Tanya, "you need protection!"

"I ain't planning to do anything bad," said Sha'Tanya, raising her hands in a defensive posture, "just play some games, eat some snacks and watch a 'flim'."

"You might be planning to watch a film and have harmless fun," said Laurel, getting into Sha'Tanya's face, "but you ain't sure what his endgame is."

"He never said or did anything inappropriate before," replied Sha'Tanya, rolling her eyes, "why would he start now?"

"You never see a whole shark coming," said Laurel, shaking her index finger at Sha'Tanya, "just the fin on his back."

Sha'Tanya paused. She knew that Laurel neither liked nor trusted Dashawn. She also knew that Laurel was a true friend, who had proven herself on more than one occasion. This was the first warning of trouble to come; if only she had taken heed. She didn't want to fight with Laurel over this matter, but she wasn't prepared to give up her plans either.

"Look, maybe you're right, maybe you're wrong, either way, I appreciate you looking out for me," she said, finally, "just be nice to Dashawn, and let's get through the day."

Laurel agreed to be amicable with Dashawn, and the conversation changed to Sha'Tanya's archnemesis, Emelia Harris' fake ponytail.

After a thirty-minute wait, a pretty bus, with side skirts, roof racks and red window tint entered the yard, and deposited a dark, well-toned boy, of average height, in blue jeans and a white brand name shirt, with a gold chain and a backpack—Dashawn had arrived.

"Big man, the meeting time was thirty minutes ago," cried Laurel, as Sha'Tanya stared dreamily at the partially chiselled Greek sculpture before her.

"The bus that came was ugly," said Dashawn, in a matter-of-fact manner, "so I had to wait till something proper came."

"Unbelievable!" cried Laurel.

"Relax, Laurel," cried Sha'Tanya, finally recovering from the sight of Dashawn, "you expect the boy to risk getting tetanus on one of those rust-bucket buses?"

"Let's just get this DVD and get out of town," said Laurel, rolling her eyes.

Fifteen minutes later, after a brief detour to Heather's Hair & Beyond for hair gel, the three teenagers were in a tiled alley with vendors on both sides of the walkway. They stopped by a dark, thick man, with flared nostrils, several white patches in his thick, black, matted hair, and a white-spotted black shirt. He had two big pieces of wood, with short shelves carrying several bootleg DVD movies. Laurel picked up a DVD and showed it to Sha'Tanya.

"Error!" cried Sha'Tanya. "I ain't watching that foolish 'flim'."

"This film is not foolish," cried Laurel, "you need more sophistication."

"I can't understand how a girl that's so big and strong, could be so sappy," said Sha'Tanya, wrinkling her face in disgust as she took an alternative DVD from the shelf."

"You gotta be drunk," cried Laurel, looking at the *Celestial Soldiers* DVD in Sha'Tanya's hand with disgust, "I can't understand how a girl that can't fight, could like so much action."

"We'll let Dashawn decide," said Sha'Tanya, looking around and realising that Dashawn was preoccupied at the other DVD display. "Earth to Dashawn!"

The girls held up their respective movie choices for Dashawn to make a decision.

"That ain't even a choice," he said, "*Celestial Soldiers*, hands down."

"As if you would say something else," Laurel muttered, as she returned her selection to the shelf.

Sha'Tanya paid for the movie, and the group started to walk away.

Suddenly, Sha'Tanya heard the vendor's voice shouting after them.

"Hold it there," he cried, "you three thieving

brats!"

Sha'Tanya was about to turn and respond, when Dashawn interjected.

"Now would be a good time to run," he cried, as he darted off.

Sha'Tanya and Laurel looked at each other quizzically, as the vendor darted towards their position. There was no time to deliberate; Sha'Tanya and Laurel darted off behind Dashawn. The teens dashed out of the alley and onto the busy sidewalk of a major road. Sha'Tanya wasn't sure what was going on, but in that moment, she was looking out for herself; she wasn't about to be caught by this angry vendor.

"Split up!" shouted Dashawn, as he dashed through another alley.

"Meet you in the yard," said Laurel, as she dashed through yet another alley, leaving Sha'Tanya on the major road.

Sha'Tanya looked back and made the startling discovery that the vendor had chosen to follow her. In Sha'Tanya's perception, with his flared nostrils, white-patched hair and white-spotted black shirt, he was just two horns short of looking like a bull charging after her. She immediately starting to zig and zag through startled pedestrians. Clad in her red top, it was like a scene from a rodeo—a bull fighter baiting a raging bull. Whenever she looked behind her, the bull was in sight—closer than he was before. She feared it was only a matter of time before he caught up, and decided that desperate measures were in order.

As Sha'Tanya approached the end of the block, she

saw pedestrians crossing the street on a zebra crossing. The waning flow of pedestrians on the crossing told her that the signal was about to change. This was perfect.

Sha'Tanya dashed onto the zebra crossing just as the stop signal was about to be displayed. The stop signal appeared as she was halfway in the crossing. As the traffic started moving, Sha'Tanya ran like she had never run before, dashing to the sidewalk on the other side of the road as drivers compressed their horns. As she reached the pavement, she was just in time to see the bull scampering back to safety on the other side of the road; he had attempted to follow her but was nearly ploughed by a bus. Sha'Tanya cut her eyes at the vendor as the bus passed. By the time the bus had passed, she was gone.

Minutes later, the teens were rendezvousing in the bus yard.

"What the blackbird just happened?" cried Laurel, as Sha'Tanya tried to catch her breath.

Dashawn just reached into his shirt and pulled out a DVD with a grin.

"Error!" cried Sha'Tanya.

"So, while we were arguing about which movie to buy," started Laurel, after breathing deeply, "you were stealing one?"

"Well, we couldn't buy this one; it's rated 'R'," replied Dashawn, in a matter-of-fact manner.

"You think that makes it better?" cried Laurel with her hands fisted at her sides. "What kind of girls you think we are?"

"Lighten up, 'Thickness'," replied Dashawn, raising his hands in a defensive posture, "nothing we can't handle—language, violence, nudity, se ..."

Before Dashawn could finish his sentence, Laurel gripped him by the neck and pinned him against one of the many vending kiosks in the bus yard.

"You will respect my friend," cried Laurel, pulling him off the kiosk and quickly slamming him back into it, "and you will not call me 'Thickness'!"

"Let him go, Laurel," cried Sha'Tanya, in alarm, as curious spectators gathered, "you're starting to cause a scene."

"He's the one that caused a scene; he put both of us in danger," cried Laurel, slamming his body into the kiosk again, as he tried to loosen her grip to no avail. "What would have happened if we couldn't outrun that vendor?"

"Sorry," said Dashawn, with what little air was able to pass through his throat.

"He said he was sorry," cried Sha'Tanya, gripping the arm with which Laurel was gripping Dashawn, "and you said you would make an effort to get along with him."

"I can't do this anymore," cried Laurel, releasing Dashawn and stepping back, staring at Sha'Tanya as the crowd began to disperse, "I ain't going anywhere with him, so either you tell him to go back home, or I'm out!"

This was a pivotal decision for Sha'Tanya, one that would alter the course of the day significantly. Could she risk losing her bodyguard? She trusted her own intentions, and she trusted Laurel's intentions, but how confident could she be about Dashawn's intentions? He was a year older than she was, and shared many interests in common; how different could his intentions really be?

As Laurel stared at her, awaiting an answer, Sha'Tanya just held her head down, unable to look Laurel in the eyes.

"Unbelievable!" cried Laurel, arms akimbo.

"Look, you didn't want to come anyway," said Sha'Tanya, finally mustering the courage to hold her head up, "you don't have to give up your day off on account of me; I will be good."

"You just don't get it," cried Laurel, with a quizzical expression, as if trying to understand Sha'Tanya's thought process, "I have more respect for you than you have for yourself!"

Sha'Tanya just held her head down.

"Have a nice day with your chiselled, thieving, womanizing, troublemaking boyfriend," said Laurel, as she walked away, deeper into the bus yard, "but don't say I didn't warn you."

"Sorry 'bout that," Sha'Tanya said, finally looking in Dashawn's direction.

"It's cool, 'Sugar Apple'," he replied, with a smooth voice, "the fact that you chose me over her makes it worth the trouble."

Before Sha'Tanya could respond, a pretty bus pulled into the yard, with side skirts, roof racks and purple window tint.

"That's our ride," said Sha'Tanya.

A couple minutes later, passengers had disembarked, and the teens stepped into the bus. They made their way through the purple and black interior, and seated themselves in the right corner of the black upholstered back seat. The upholstery was trimmed with purple, to match the window tint, and behind every seat was a plaque, airbrushed with a purple mist, and the words, "Speed Demon" in white.

"Nice ride," said Dashawn.

"You know I only ride in the best," said Sha'Tanya, with a smug grin.

"Of course," said Dashawn, with a smile, "only the best for the best."

Sha'Tanya blushed as she stared into the eyes of this Greek sculpture in the making. In that moment, she resolved that it would be a very good day, and that she had made the correct decision. Whether or not that was a true assessment, she would find out in due course.

One hour later, Sha'Tanya was standing in front of an orange and brown, wooden house with a small veranda at the front. She led Dashawn up a very short flight of steps, and through the veranda to the front door. Her mother had already left for work and she had the house all to herself.

"Welcome to my house," said Sha'Tanya, as she unlocked the door and led Dashawn into a cosy living room. There was a mahogany suite consisting of a three-seater, a two-seater and a one-seater chair, set around a small centre table, facing a television set on a neat mahogany stand.

After the teens removed their shoes, Sha'Tanya led Dashawn to the three-seater, where she motioned for him to sit. She then disappeared into the kitchen, returning shortly after with two bowls, one with popcorn and one with potato chips. She returned to see the DVD Dashawn had stolen on the centre table.

"You brought the drinks?" she asked, as she put the snacks on the centre table.

Dashawn entered his backpack and retrieved four plastic soda bottles which he placed on the table.

"You sure you want to watch this 'flim'?" she asked, pointing at the R-rated DVD on the table.

"Well, yeah," said Dashawn, in a matter-of-fact manner, "but I ain't gonna think any less of you if you can't handle *Wicked Weaponry*; we could watch the *Celestial Soldiers* movie."

Sha'Tanya cut her eyes at Dashawn, before snatching the DVD off the table and popping it into the DVD player, which sat on a small shelf under the television set. She had been really looking forward to watching *Celestial Soldiers* with Dashawn, but she didn't want her new boyfriend to think she was less mature than he was.

After turning on the television set and starting the DVD, Sha'Tanya proceeded to make herself comfortable next to Dashawn in the middle of the three-seater. As the opening titles for the movie were displayed, she grabbed a soda from the centre table, and proceeded to open it.

"Really?" she asked, looking at the bottle quizzically.

"What?"

"This is a flat drink; there's supposed to be a hiss

when I open it," she said, "it ain't even bubbly—error!"

"No error," said Dashawn, looking at her with a smile, "taste it."

Sha'Tanya lifted the drink to her head, before pausing and giving Dashawn a critical look.

"Boy, you put alcohol in these bottles?"

"Well, yeah," said Dashawn, in a matter-of-fact manner, as he took another bottle off the table, "but I ain't gonna think any less of you if you can't handle it; I brought a regular soda just in case."

Sha'Tanya paused for a moment. She didn't want her new boyfriend to think she was less mature than he was, but she had never had alcohol and wasn't about to start.

"It's a bit too early for that," she said, as she returned the bottle to the table, and took the soda from Dashawn.

Just then, her attention was snapped back to the movie when a character on the screen began to swear repeatedly. This gave Sha'Tanya an uneasy feeling; her mother and father used fowl language sometimes, as did some of her neighbours, but she had always had a clear understanding that such language was not appropriate for someone her age to use, or even listen to. However, she didn't want Dashawn to think she was less mature than he was, especially after backing out of drinking the alcohol. She resolved to ignore the expletives and act as though she was accustomed to it.

In short order, another source of uneasiness presented itself. Dashawn pulled a lighter out of his pocket, along with a joint.

"Big man, that's weed you got in my house?" asked Sha'Tanya, staring intently at Dashawn.

"Well, yeah," said Dashawn, in a matter-of-fact manner.

"You had plans of lighting that in here?" started Sha'Tanya, before Dashawn could say anything else.

"No problem, 'Sugar Apple'," said Dashawn, in a smooth voice, as he put away the joint and the lighter, "I ain't addicted or anything like that; if you don't want me to smoke, I don't have to smoke."

"It ain't even 'bout me," started Sha'Tanya, uneasy about the smoking but still trying to appear more mature, "when my mother gets back home, in here would smell like a drug den—error!"

"That's cool," said Dashawn, with a smile, "all I need to enjoy this day is your company."

Sha'Tanya smiled and resumed watching the movie. As Dashawn sipped his alcohol, and more and more expletives from the movie pierced her ears, Laurel's words echoed in her mind.

"Have a nice day with your chiselled, thieving, womanizing, troublemaking boyfriend, but don't say I didn't warn you … you never see a whole shark coming, just the fin on his back … you ain't sure what his endgame is."

Now, as she sat alone with him, after dismissing her bodyguard, she nervously hoped that she had made the right decision. He had done many inappropriate things already—things which she had never been exposed to before that day. However, he had also been very understanding, never forcing his desires upon her, so she took comfort in that fact and tried to relax.

Suddenly, a character in the movie started to kill a group of people in the most gruesome and graphic ways imaginable. Sha'Tanya couldn't hide her discomfort, as she returned her soda to the table, unable to continue drinking it. Dashawn returned his alcoholic beverage to the table as well, then came closer to her.

"It's alright, sweet girl," he whispered as he put his toned arm around her, "I'm here for you."

For a moment, Sha'Tanya felt comforted in the embrace of Dashawn's chiselled biceps. She was fully comfortable with his arm around her but she wasn't prepared for what happened next.

The character in the movie concluded his killing spree, and proceeded to remove his blood-stained clothes—all of them. Suddenly, the embrace which had brought Sha'Tanya comfort, became a source of discomfort. She had never seen such nudity, and the visual took her mind to a place it had never been before. The innocence of her present situation began to disintegrate and she realised that being close to someone could have different meanings to different people.

Her thought process was suddenly shattered, as she felt Dashawn's other hand on her leg. The discomfort which came upon her was unapparelled. Her heart skipped a beat as fear, anxiety and shame pierced it all at once. The entire morning, she had tried to be more grownup for Dashawn, but not this grownup; a line had to be drawn.

"Error," she cried, as she grabbed his hand and lifted it off her leg, "that ain't for that purpose!"

"You can't be serious," he cried, gripping her firmly with the arm which was still around her, "I was patient with you the whole morning but this is taking a joke too far; stop being selfish."

"Selfish?" cried Sha'Tanya, staring at him with discombobulation. "Big man, this is my leg!"

"You plan to just leave it there, to get cobwebs?" cried Dashawn. "Other people gotta use that too!"

"Screws loose in your head?" cried Sha'Tanya, as she broke the embrace and jumped up off the chair.

"Calm down, sweet girl," said Dashawn, smoothly, while still seated, "I'm sorry. I was just so excited to be close to you, I got carried away."

"Carried away?" cried Sha'Tanya, giving him a critical stare with her arms folded. "You mean you got kidnapped!"

"Sit back down, sweet girl," replied Dashawn, calmly, as he patted the cushion next to him, "we would just make out, and leave your leg out of it."

"Error!" cried Sha'Tanya, full of apprehension. "I never kissed a boy in my life and I ain't looking to start today!"

"You can't be serious!" cried Dashawn, jumping up from the chair. "You're supposed to be my girlfriend; what you expected to do here today?"

"Relax, hang out, watch a movie, play some games and talk," said Sha'Tanya, raising her hands in a defensive posture.

"Girl, you could do that with anybody," cried Dashawn, walking towards Sha'Tanya as she stepped backwards, "that ain't what a boyfriend is for. We have a contract."

"What contract?" cried Sha'Tanya, as she stepped backward into a wall, "I ain't promise you anything."

"From the time you invited me to spend the day alone, you promised me something," said Dashawn, stepping forward and grabbing Sha'Tanya's hands firmly, "and I ain't leaving here without it!"

"Let me go," said Sha'Tanya, struggling to break free of his grip to no avail.

"Not till you kiss me," he cried, tightening his grip, "you belong to me!"

Sha'Tanya started to panic inside, as fear and anxiety lit a fire inside her. She had no bodyguard, and no backup; she was left to her own devices. Thinking quickly, she raised her knee with force, jamming it into Dashawn's groin.

"Error!" she shouted, as Dashawn immediately released his grip, and fell to the floor, groaning in pain.

Sha'Tanya wasted no time in dashing for the front door.

"You had better get your things, and leave," she cried, looking at Dashawn as she opened the door.

Dashawn eventually rose from the floor, but the look in his eyes told her that he wasn't looking to round up his belongings. There was fire in his eyes as he clenched his fists and huffed heavily. Whatever trust Sha'Tanya had placed in him before, was now obliterated, and as he charged towards her, she dashed through the open door and a chase ensued—the second one for the morning.

"This is bad" she thought, as she fled down the deserted street, with her bare feet, "nobody's home; I am entirely on my own."

Earlier that morning, she had been counting on these factors, to provide the perfect environment for a good time. Now, however, these were the very factors providing the perfect environment for her pursuer to have his way.

As she approached the main road, she saw a couple of cars and a bus pass. She looked behind her to discover that Dashawn was gaining on her and conceded that the main road was her only hope; it wasn't as busy as it had been earlier that morning, but there was still some activity, and someone might see her plight and intervene.

Sha'Tanya ran out of her street and onto the main road to be greeted by a shocking sight—it was Laurel. She had seemingly just disembarked the bus which Sha'Tanya had seen a moment ago. There was no time for clarification; Sha'Tanya dashed behind Laurel as Dashawn came onto the scene and stopped in his tracks.

The teens now stood on a sidewalk, with a main road on one side, and a wall on the next. Dashawn stood with bare feet, facing Laurel, several metres away, as Sha'Tanya fortified herself behind Laurel.

"This ain't concern you, Laurel," shouted Dashawn, "step aside before I manhandle you!"

"Relax yourself, little boy," cried Laurel, arms akimbo, "I would hit you so hard, you would wake up yesterday!"

ENDGAME

Sha'Tanya watched from behind Laurel, as Dashawn grabbed a big rock off the ground, darted forward and hurled it at Laurel. As Sha'Tanya instinctively ducked, she watched in disbelief as Laurel charged forward, caught the big rock and hurled it back at Dashawn with incredible force. Dashawn narrowly managed to dodge the rock, which flew past him to hit a stop sign behind him, and shattered into uncountable fragments.

Dashawn then charged at Laurel and propelled himself into the air to deliver an airborne kick. Sha'Tanya looked on in disbelief as Laurel narrowly moved her body out of his path, gripped his foot as it zoomed past her and spun his body around in a semicircle before releasing the foot and sending him flying through the air. Dashawn's body hit the ground with a thud. As he started to pick himself up, Laurel charged at him like an elephant defending its young. Dashawn scampered to his feet and took off in the opposite direction.

Minutes later, back at the house, Sha'Tanya sat on her couch in total shambles, weeping bitterly. She felt stupid and ashamed, and she was scared to even imagine how much worse her situation could have been. As she sat there, wishing she had taken a different path, the events of that day flashed before her mind's eye like a movie.

Suddenly, she felt a hand around her and heard Laurel's voice in her ear.

"I got rid of the alcohol and the DVD."

Sha'Tanya looked around at Laurel—who had seated herself next to her—with tears in her eyes.

"I don't deserve a friend like you," she said, "I don't

even know how to thank you."

"I couldn't relax knowing that you could be in danger," Laurel replied, softly. "You can thank me by learning from your mistakes."

"Believe me, I ain't ending up in this position ever again," said Sha'Tanya, drying her eyes and face, "I wanted to be grownup so bad, that I made stupid decisions and ignored good advice; today showed me that I ain't ready for that grownup life."

"So, no more Dashawn?"

"Correct!"

"No more older boys?"

"Correct! No boys, period—for now."

"No more ignoring my advice?"

"Correct!"

"And you would be cool with people calling you a little girl, now?"

Sha'Tanya paused, giving Laurel a critical stare.

"I appreciate this girl with every fibre in my body, but I am also allergic to foolishness," she thought, before expressing the sentiment in a single, concise word.

"Error!"

Sha'Tanya UNDONE

The only constant in childhood is change. Barbadian schoolgirl, Sha'Tanya Carter is definitely feeling the effects of change—both good and bad; she goes from fourteen to fifteen, from third form to fourth form, from a happy life to one of turmoil.

After a fateful hurricane throws her into deep poverty, Sha'Tanya becomes obsessed with keeping her new reality a secret. For two years, she goes to any length to keep her image intact, including mixing with undesirables, trespassing and malicious conduct. These efforts do not go according to plan, and Sha'Tanya learns that extreme actions to avoid shame, often lead to shame in other areas.

When trying to preserve one's pride, what measures are reasonable? How far is too far? What price is too high?

Make your own conclusions as you follow the traumatic, tumultuous events which threaten to leave Sha'Tanya undone.

Sha'Tanya also appears in the *Adrian* Series

www.marioherbert.com